## Looking at

# Animals in
# RIVERS
## and
# LAKES

Published by Raintree Steck-Vaughn Publishers,
an imprint of Steck-Vaughn Company

**Series Editor** Honor Head
**Series Designer** Hayley Cove
**Picture Researcher** Juliet Duff
**Map Artwork** Robin Carter / Wildlife Art Agency
**Animal Symbols** Arlene Adams

**Raintree Steck-Vaughn Publishers Staff**
**Project Manager:** Joyce Spicer
**Editor:** Pam Wells
**Cover Design:** Gino Coverty

**Library of Congress Cataloging-in-Publication Data**
Butterfield, Moira, 1961–
Animals in rivers and lakes / Moira Butterfield.
p. cm. — (Looking at —)
Includes index.
Summary: Introduces animals that live in rivers, lakes, streams, and ponds, including the trout, kingfisher, crocodile, and bullfrog.
ISBN 0-7398-0108-2
1. Freshwater animals — Juvenile literature. [1. Freshwater animals.]
I. Title. II. Series: Butterfield, Moira, 1961– Looking at —
QL 141.B88    1999
578.76 — dc21                98-53204
CIP    AC

Printed in China
1 2 3 4 5 6 7 8 9 0 LB 02 01 00 99

**Photographic credits**
Frank Lane Picture Agency: 6 Gerard Lascz; 9 F Polking; 13 F Merlet; 19 D Braud/Dembinsky; 21 Roger Tidman; 26 Derek Middleton; 28 Treat Davidson. NHPA: 16,17 A.N.T; 18 Dan Griggs; 20 Nigel J Dennis; 24 Stephen Dalton. Oxford Scientific Films: 7 Breck P Kent; 8 G A Maclean; 10 Daniel J Fox; 11 Alan and Sandy Carey; 12 Max Gibbons; 27 Presse-Tige Pictures. Planet Earth Pictures: 14, 15, Jonathan Scott; 22 Peter Scoones; 23 Petr Velensky; 25 Andrew McGeeney; 29 Ken Lucas.
**Cover credit** Otter: Oxford Scientific Films/Daniel J Fox

# Looking at

# Animals in
# RIVERS
## and
# LAKES

## Moira Butterfield

**RSVP**
**RAINTREE**
**STECK-VAUGHN**
P U B L I S H E R S
A Steck-Vaughn Company

*Austin, Texas*

www.steck-vaughn.com

# Introduction

Rivers, lakes, streams, and ponds are freshwater places. This means the water is not salty as it would be in an ocean or a sea. There are freshwater places all over the world.

Lots of animals of all shapes and sizes live in or around rivers and lakes. There are tiny insects, strange-looking fish, colorful birds, and even big, fierce animals, such as crocodiles.

All these animals have their own ways of living in freshwater places.

# Contents

# Trout

Trout swim along in rivers and lakes looking for small fish and tadpoles to gobble up. Fishers like to catch trout because they are good to eat.

Female trout lay tiny eggs on the riverbed. The baby fish that hatch from the eggs are called fry.

# Kingfisher

A kingfisher is a brightly colored little bird that lives by streams. It sits on a branch above the water waiting for a fish to swim by. Then, it dives beneath the surface and spears or grabs the fish with its beak. It also uses its beak to peck a hole for its nest in the riverbank.

# Otter

Otters are good swimmers. They are fast enough to catch fish, and they will eat frogs and birds, too. Otters make squeaking noises to each other.

When they are not hunting, otters like to play together on the riverbank. Baby otters are called kits.

# Catfish

There are lots of different freshwater catfish, big and small. They look as if they have cat's whiskers. But these are really long, thin feelers called barbels. As the fish swim along the riverbed, they use their barbels to feel through the mud for food to eat.

# Crocodile

Crocodiles live in warm parts of the world. They float silently in rivers and water holes looking for animals to catch and eat. They have thick, scaly skin and sharp teeth.

Sometimes crocodiles crawl onto the riverbank to sunbathe. They may come to lay eggs in a nest they have dug.

# Platypus

This strange-looking creature lives in Australia. It has a beak like a duck, silky, soft fur, and four big feet that look like paddles. When it dives under water, it closes its eyes and ears. Then, it uses its beak to feel along the riverbed for food. It eats crabs, snails, and worms.

# Beaver

Beavers gnaw through trees with their sharp teeth. They use the branches to build a big wall across the river where they live. This is called a dam.

Behind the dam, the water spreads out to become a big pool. The beavers build a nest of twigs to live in, called a lodge.

# Heron

The tall heron stands as still as a statue in ponds and pools. It waits for fish or frogs to swim by. This bird stands so quietly that the fish do not notice the danger until it is too late. Then, the heron thrusts its sharp beak down quickly and snatches the fish from the water.

# Crab

Freshwater crabs are hard to spot because they hide among pond weeds or under stones. On their front legs, they have large claws that they use for eating.

When they come out to look for food, they walk sideways. Female crabs lay lots of little eggs that hatch as tiny baby crabs.

# Dragonfly

Dragonflies live near ponds and streams looking for other insects to catch and eat. They have very big eyes, two pairs of thin wings, and a fierce-looking mouth for biting their food. Dragonflies can hover in the air, turn around, or dive down quickly to chase something.

# Water Vole

Water voles live on riverbanks. They look like mice, but they are much better swimmers. They are always busy, running here and there, looking for food.

They build themselves a cosy riverside nest lined with grass. Here they can hide from hungry enemies, such as owls.

# Bullfrog

Bullfrogs can live in the water and on land. They have long, powerful back legs that they use to jump high in the air. They also have webbed feet for swimming. Bullfrogs have bulging eyes and make a loud croaking noise. Females lay black and white eggs near the top of the water.

# Where They Live

This map of the world shows you where the animals live.

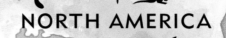

**NORTH AMERICA**

**SOUTH AMERICA**

 trout

kingfisher

otter

catfish

crocodile

platypus

beaver

heron

crab

dragonfly

water vole

bullfrog

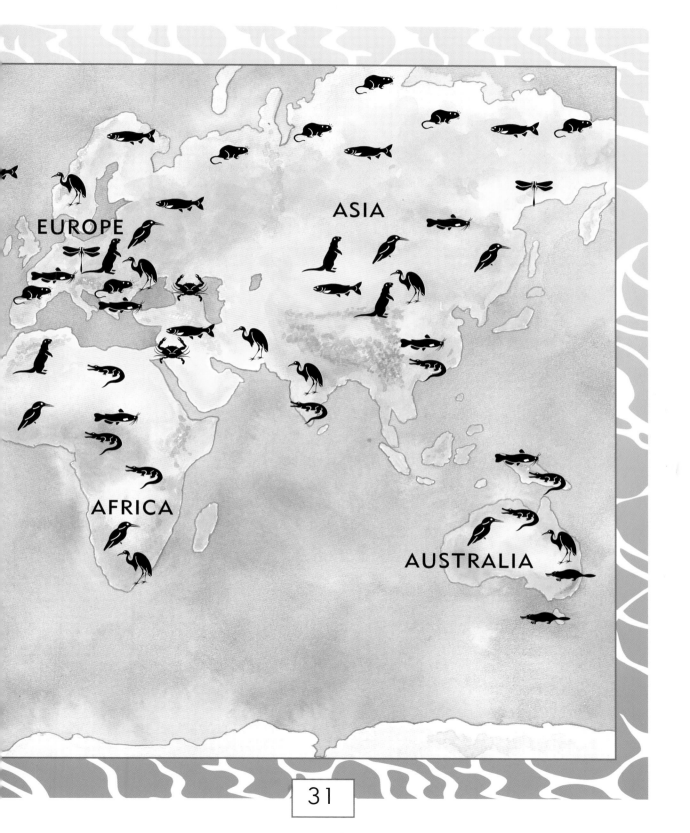

EUROPE

ASIA

AFRICA

AUSTRALIA

# Index of Words to Learn

**hatch** To be born from an egg. . . . . . . . 7, 23

**hover** To hang in the air without moving
backward or forward. . . . . . . . . . . . 25

**riverbank** The side of a river. It is often
made of mud. . . . . . . . . . . . . . 9, 11, 15

**riverbed** The bottom of a river. It can
be muddy or stony. . . . . . . . . . . 7, 13, 17

**stream** A small river. . . . . . . . . . . 9, 25

**water hole** A big pond. . . . . . . . . . . 15

**webbed feet** Feet with pieces of skin between
the toes. They help an animal to swim. . . . 29